THE PRESENCE

A NOVELLA

BY

KAREN E. TAYLOR

OTHER BOOKS BY KAREN E. TAYLOR

THE VAMPIRE LEGACY SERIES:

Blood Red Dawn

Thirst

Crave

Hunger

CELLAR

MEXICAN MOON & OTHER STORIES

LOVE AND MONSTERS

THE PRESENCE

Copyright © 2015 Karen E. Taylor

THE PRESENCE first saw print in shorter form in SEDUCTIVE
SPECTRES, published by Masquerade Books, 1996.
The story was reprinted in FANGS AND ANGEL WINGS, published
by Betancourt & Company, in 2003, and has been updated for this
newest version.

Cover Design Copyright ©2016 Karen E. Taylor

Karen E. Taylor
Alexandria, VA
http://www.karenetaylor.com

THE PRESENCE

I remember that first day as the turning point, as one of the most beautiful days of my life. The sun shone warmly, it could almost have been summer except for the cold wind that blew my long blonde hair into a cloud of tangles. But it was spring and the earth seemed to be bursting with vitality. I felt that if I stood in one place too long, its infectious growth would flow up my limbs and I would take root like—*oh, what the hell was her name... Apollo and... and... oh, yeah*—"Daphne."

"Miss Hawthorne?"

I jumped slightly and glanced at Jonathan Weber, my future landlord, scarcely realizing I had spoken. Not wanting him to think I was too eccentric—*he's no Apollo, but he might do in a pinch*—I pushed the hair from my eyes and gave him a warm smile. "Nothing, I was just sort of thinking out loud. I'm sorry, you were saying?"

He was substantially taller than I, probably at least a foot, and his dark hair, only slightly grey, was tousled from the wind. His brown eyes danced as he became aware of my scrutiny and he returned my smile encouragingly. "I said that the utility bills are generally higher in the winter. With all those windows..." he shrugged and pointed to the third floor apartment of the Victorian-style home. "But of course, that's why you want it. The light is wonderful for painting. I believe it was used by the original owner as a studio, also."

I looked to where the sunlight glinted from the row of windows and felt a shiver of anticipation. "It's perfect," I whispered to myself and my fingers tingled, aching for the brush, the smooth, sensuous sweep of oil across canvas. "Let's go up," I tugged on his sleeve like an impatient child, "I want to see the inside."

He began to climb an outer set of stairs and I followed eagerly. The entrance to the enclosed set of stairs was unlocked and he opened the door and paused on the landing. "You can lock this if you want; the couple living in the second floor apartment," and he gestured to a closed door opposite the entrance, "have a complete set of keys. I expect it probably seems strange, with you coming from a big city like New York, but many people around here still leave their doors open. We've very little crime here, even though the town has expanded a bit." He shrugged and smiled at me, then climbed the last flight of stairs, opening the door to my new apartment and holding it back to allow me to enter first.

Five more steps up and I was there. The first thing I noticed was the smell of fresh paint and new carpeting. Underneath those odors I thought I detected a heady floral scent, exotic and seductive. And despite the wash of sunlight coming through the windows, the room was cold, icy cold. I walked into the living area, folding my arms across my chest so that the tightening of my nipples would not be so obvious.

The apartment was ideal, not as compact as the place I had moved from, and not large enough to be a burden. The kitchen, though small, had been completely modernized, as had the bath. The bedroom was merely a curtained alcove adjacent to the main area. But the studio was well-lit, airy and exactly as he had described it to me. Once again I felt the urge to begin painting at once, even though the bulk of my supplies would not arrive until tomorrow.

Jonathan cleared his throat nervously and I turned, surprised to see that he was still standing at the top of the stairs, not completely in the apartment. "This is a wonderful place," I said, "I just can't believe my luck in finding it vacant. Thank you."

"Well," he smiled hesitantly, "it's like I tried to explain to you in our correspondence, not too many people have felt comfortable here. I really hope it's different for you."

"You've never been to New York, have you?"

He shook his head, "No, but what has that got to do with anything?"

My laughter seemed to puzzle him, so I continued. "Well, compared to the places I've been, the people I've roomed with and the sights I've seen, your ghost should be a welcome change." I tried unsuccessfully to hide my skepticism. I did not believe in ghosts. "So tell me, does he appear at midnight, moaning and clanking his chains? Or does he just throw sharp objects at the people who intrude in his space?"

He shook his head with vehemence, almost indignantly. "No, of course not. It's really nothing like that; if it were I would close the place off, or," and his face held the trace of a smile, "maybe I'd sell tickets. I don't know if I would even go so far as to call it a ghost; at the most it's a presence, or maybe just the residue of strong emotions. No one, to my knowledge, has ever seen anything. People stay for a few months, then find a reason to leave. It's never anything specific."

"Whatever it is, I'm not worried about it. So don't you worry either. I'll be fine, honestly. And I'd feel quite at home if only it were just a bit warmer."

"Oh, God, I'm sorry. I can fix that up pretty quickly." He seemed to relax finally and walked across the room to the radiator. "Like I said, Miss Hawthorne, I hope you'll stay," he glanced over at me shyly while he adjusted the heat, "it's an honor to have a beautiful and talented artist staying here."

"Call me Mara," I said, suddenly embarrassed at his compliment, and was startled to hear the name whispered back to me.

He gave the radiator a kick with his foot, "You'll get used to this thing after a while. It makes a lot of noise sometimes." As if in response to his statement, the radiator hissed again, a close enough approximation of my name that I realized what had happened.

I laughed as he moved to the steps, "You know, Jonathan, I don't think you have a ghost at all; just a noisy heating system."

"Maybe," he gestured to the telephone, "but if you have any trouble, please give me a call. My number's on a card next to the phone. And I do live on the first floor, so if you have an emergency, you can just run down and get me." He walked over to me and extended his hand. I shook it; he had a nice grip, firm but gentle and I felt that he held my hand just a little bit longer than necessary.

"Thank you, Jonathan. I'm sure everything will be fine."

"Do you want some help with your stuff?" Although he had been reluctant about coming into the apartment now it seemed that he didn't want to leave. I wondered if he enjoyed my company that much, or if he was just concerned about the ghost making an appearance and frightening off a steady rental income.

"No, thanks anyway. All I have is a small suitcase and my ipod. Everything else should arrive tomorrow. And since I won't be sleeping here tonight, I think I'll just look around a bit more and head over to the motel."

"Did I warn you about the connectivity problems here?"

I smiled at him. "Yes, several times during our correspondence. And as I said, I'm good with that. For a while, anyway. I don't own a television set, I cancelled my cell phone contract before leaving the city, and closed down all of my email and social accounts."

Jonathan winced. "That seems a bit drastic."

I nodded. "But a fresh start isn't fresh if you drag around all of the old shit with you, is it?" I didn't feel obligated to give him an explanation. He didn't need to know the hell of past relationships I was escaping. But I smiled again. "Anyway, I'm sure there are places I can use the Internet if I need to."

"Sure, lots of them." He hesitated a second and the temperature seemed to drop again. Jonathan shook his head and headed to the door. "Okay then, you take care."

I followed him and he turned around and handed me two sets of keys. "Here you go," he said, "I guess I'll see you around." He walked out, closed the door behind him and I was alone.

Pushing the keys into the back pocket of my jeans, I slowly walked into the studio. Sheer lace curtains that diffused the sunlight and traced delicate shadowy webs on the walls and tiled floor covered the wide expanse of windows, flanking the long wall of the room. Beneath the windows was a long upholstered bench; I sat down and pulled the curtains to one side. I was relieved to see that there were no houses across the street, just an overgrown swatch of trees and brush. "Good," I said aloud, "then there's no one to spy on me when I want to paint in the nude." Shivering, I realized that there would be no nudity here until the heat improved. I rubbed my hands up and down the raised flesh on my arms and, rising from the window seat, went into the other room to check out the closets.

They were more than adequate; my wardrobe was almost completely limited to jeans, t-shirts and sweaters, including only two dresses for gallery appearances and the like. My life style was Bohemian, but it suited me fine.

I stopped in the bathroom and tried out the plumbing. When I finished, I could again smell the floral scent I had first noted. When I explored the kitchen, the mystery solved itself. Lying on the window ledge, at the end of the dormer, was a single rose, open and fragrant. "How nice," I said as I picked it up and inhaled. "I'll have to remember to thank Jonathan."

"Ahhraa..." the radiator hissed again as I walked past it on my way to the door.

"Don't worry," I whispered, patting the ironwork with a grin for my foolishness, "you just get this place warm and I'll be back tomorrow."

The movers were late. I had arrived as agreed by eight, and after unpacking what clothes and few toiletries I carried with me, waited by the windows in the studio. I was slightly hung over from an evening spent discussing modern art with the bartender at my motel. For someone living in this backwater town, he had proven to be fairly well versed with some of my more popular compatriots; this surprised me until I found out that he was a graduate student from a university in a nearby town. And when he discovered that I did representational art, not "those godawful paint splatters," he had kept my glass filled until the bar closed.

He'd wanted to come back to my room, but I slept alone, having learned the hard way not to trust my judgment about men after a few drinks. That was the way I had become involved with so many men, especially my ex-husband; he was the main reason I'd moved from the city, hoping for an escape from his continual leeching of my money, my self-respect, and my emotional reserves.

I stretched a bit, having become cramped sitting and watching out the windows, sorry that my thoughts had brought me back to past relationships. "Okay, you bastards," I said with a bitter laugh, shifting my position to lay down flat on the window seat, "just try and find me here." I crossed my arms behind my head and studied the shadows of the lace curtains on the ceiling. The sun streaming through the windows warmed my face, soothed my throbbing head, and lulled me to sleep.

Somehow my thoughts of gods the day before became twisted up with my musings about the men I had known. I was Daphne and they took turns as Apollo, chasing me, leading me back to this apartment, strangely furnished and heavily scented with the overpowering aroma of a thousand roses. When he caught me, it seemed different somehow, because he was different and everything was finally okay. He promised me, oh, he promised me so much, all I had ever wanted, an eternity of love and fidelity.

"Forever, Mara," he whispered, his breath causing the hair on the back of my neck to rise, causing delicate shivers to undulate through my willing body. "This will be forever."

"Yes," I agreed and moaned as his hands caressed my breasts through my thin shirt, teasing the nipples to an aching erectness. "You're cold," I murmured, "you are so cold."

"But you will warm me, my lovely one." His hands fumbled with the zipper of my jeans and, in spite of their icy touch, I felt the answering gush of warmth from within me. "I need you," he urged as he slid my panties down my thighs, "I love you. Give yourself to me, Mara."

"Yes," I gasped, "yes." The weight of his body on mine was exciting, yet comforting, as if it were something I had been awaiting all my life. But when I reached my arms up to pull him down to me, they found nothing. "Where are you?" I asked desperately, struggling to open my sleep-sealed eyes, "I can't touch you."

"No," he said, a heavy sadness in his voice as tangible as the fragrance and the cold, "you cannot touch me. Yet."

A loud knocking on the door woke me, and I sat up, disoriented and trembling. My jeans lay on the floor in a crumpled heap and my panties were tangled around my ankles. My shirt was bunched up around my neck and as I pulled it down I noticed the small reddened patches on my breasts. "Jesus," I swore as I hurriedly dressed to let the movers in, "that was one hell of a dream."

I waited impatiently as the movers unloaded my meager assortment of furniture. The first piece of furniture to come off the truck was my bed, an antique brass piece that had been in my family for generations. Although over the years it had undergone many renovations—the entire undercarriage had been rewired, and new springs and supports were installed—it still creaked dreadfully with even normal sleeping movements. The noise it made during more strenuous use was incredible, but I didn't really mind. Especially not here, I reminded myself, trying to shake loose of the strange, erotic dream I'd had, I haven't come to this two-bit town to pursue relationships or sex. I've come to paint.

Sitting on the edge of the bare mattress, one leg crossed under me and the other swinging free, I casually directed the placement of the rest of the furniture. The two chairs, the end table and an old lamp went into the living room, the dresser, along with another lamp, older still, to the right of my bed and the dinette table and two folding chairs, into the kitchen. Following the furniture were five cartons labeled 'miscellaneous household items' containing mostly kitchen goods and linens and two large suitcases containing my clothes. I ran my fingers idly through my tangled hair as I watched, not really caring where any of these items went. But when one of the movers came up the stairs with the first large crate marked 'canvases,' I jumped off the bed and, to the obvious disgust of the workers, became actively involved in the process of unloading.

Finally, when all my supplies had been unpacked and accounted for on the bill of lading, I signed for the shipment and the movers left. I was anxious to get started; my thoughts the other day of gods in pursuit, not to mention that incredible dream, had inspired me to start a series of mythologically-based paintings, all portraying the romance of the supernatural.

"Although, let's be realistic, Mara," I told myself as I stripped off my jeans and donned an oversized painting shirt, "romance is just a euphemistic term for what you really have in mind. What we're talking about here is lust—all those hot, sweaty bodies intertwined." Pulling a large canvas out of the stack, I laughed a little, remembering some of the reviews my last show had received from the more conservative papers. "Too much exposed flesh," one had said. And "a flagrant and graphic depiction of sexual acts, bordering on pornography," said another.

"And you know what?" I crossed the room and turned up the radiator, "I sold every stinking one of them. People were literally panting for more."

The radiator hissed out a little sigh, "Ahhraa," and I patted it.

"That's right, baby, just give me a little more heat and I'll take care of the sex."

Walking back into the studio, I paced a bit, considering the empty canvas. I decided that the first painting would be of Daphne and Apollo, since they hadn't actually consummated their relationship. That way each progressive canvas could accelerate the process ending in the ultimate seduction of... oh, hell, I don't know who, I thought, I'm going to need to do research on this sucker.

It didn't really matter, I had enough information to paint the first scene and inspiration would follow. It always did. But I made a mental note to check with Jonathan Weber about the nearest library so that I could either get a book or check online. In the meantime, I could simply concentrate on Daphne.

How would she feel, I wondered, setting out my tubes of oil and preparing a few brushes, being pursued by a god? Would she be flattered by his attention, but secure enough in herself to believe she could escape him? Wouldn't she even be just a little bit curious wondering about what it would be like, how his mouth would feel on hers, his hands on her breasts, the size of his....

"Get real, Mara," I said out loud, "she was a virgin, and had vowed to remain one. What the hell did she care about the size of the man's penis?" Snorting to myself, I began to block out the picture, mixing a delicate pink flesh color for Daphne, a darker color for Apollo's skin and sketching in suggestions of their bodies and the flowers and forest in the background.

As always I became immersed in my work and long hours passed before I stopped, suddenly conscious of the darkening windows and a gnawing hunger. The apartment seemed cold now, although my shirt was drenched with sweat. I peeled it off and went into the bathroom for a shower.

Turning the water up as hot as it would go, I let it run for a few minutes to build up the warmth in the room. I brushed my teeth while I waited, watching through the mirror as the puffs of steam billowed, eventually blocking the vision of myself. A childhood fear returned to me as I bent over the sink and rinsed my mouth, someone could be standing right behind me and I would never know. Even as I thought it, I shivered. "Jesus, Mara, you're letting this haunted house business get to you on your first night here. You've got more sense than that."

Nevertheless, I couldn't control a furtive glance over my shoulder before getting into the shower. But when the hot water hit my tired body it soothed and comforted and I relaxed as I soaped myself. When I washed my breasts, I noticed small bruises around the nipples, but dismissed them. My skin was extremely fair and delicate; I was always turning up bruised in the oddest places, never remembering what I had done to cause it.

I dried myself, took a blow dryer to my hair, and put on a clean pair of jeans and a bulky sweater. Then I picked up my keys and my purse and bounded down the many flights of stairs to the street outside. Jonathan's light was on, so I walked up the few steps of his front porch and rang his bell.

"Hi," I said, when he answered the door. "I don't mean to be a pest, but I was wondering if you could tell me where the library is in this town. And if you could point me to a good restaurant nearby, I'd be eternally grateful."

"No problem," he pulled off the pair of reading glasses he'd been wearing, stuffed them impatiently into his shirt pocket, and checked his watch. "Library's closed right now. And you don't really want to use the one in town anyway. The college's is better." He rubbed his eyes slightly, and when he looked at me again, his eyes seemed tired and red.

"I'm sorry," I said quickly, embarrassed that I had interrupted him, "did I come at a bad time?"

"No, no, not at all. I was just grading some term papers."

"Oh, you're a teacher? I didn't know that."

"I'm a professor at the college, actually. What did you think I did for a living?"

I gave him a wry smile, "I didn't really think of you having a profession. I just guessed that your leasing apartments was enough."

Jonathan laughed. "Oh, come on. Your rent isn't that high, is it? How on earth do you think I could make a living out of it?"

"Maybe I visualized you as the slum-landlord of this place."

"Thanks a lot," he said dryly.

"You're welcome." I paused a minute, then continued, "What do you teach?"

"Antiquities," he said apologetically, then shrugged, "I know, it's boring as all get out."

"No," I thought of my current fascination with mythology, and gave him a warm smile, "I don't think it's boring at all, Jonathan. But I don't want to hold you up any longer. And I'm starving."

"Let me get my coat. I'll be right with you."

"Oh, no, I didn't mean to..." I blushed slightly at the thought that he might think I was fishing for a dinner invitation.

He came back with his coat and looked at me with shy amusement. I blushed more deeply, knowing that he noticed my embarrassment. "Oh, I'm sure you didn't," he said, closing and locking his door, "but I did."

We walked three blocks into the main thoroughfare of the town and stopped at the traffic light.

"Well, what would you like to eat?" Jonathan pointed to his right, "Over here we have pizza, burgers, and health food. And," he spun around and pointed the other way, "over here is the diner, and a steak and spaghetti joint."

I looked at him with his arms out flung and began to laugh.

"What's so funny?"

"You look like the scarecrow from the Wizard of Oz."

"I do?" He looked down at himself then gave a boyish grin and dropped his arms. "Yeah, I guess I do. And you haven't even seen me fall down yet."

We stood silently for a minute waiting for the light to change. "The scarecrow, huh? Is that good?"

"Depends," I said, still chuckling to myself.

"On what?"

"On whether the diner serves an authentic cherry cola or not."

"Well, you're in luck, young lady. The diner it is."

The light changed and he tentatively put a hand on my waist as if to guide me. When I did not avoid the contact but leaned into him as we crossed, his grip grew stronger.

The diner was crowded but we got the last available booth. The server greeted him by name and he ordered our drinks first so that I could have time to look at the menu. When she brought the sodas, I tore open the straw, took one long sip and sighed in contentment.

"Authentic enough for you?"

"It's wonderful." I took another sip and went back to the menu. A shadow fell over us and I looked up to see a young girl standing hesitantly, waiting for someone to notice her.

"Dr. Weber?" Her voice cracked a bit over his name. Her hands were stuffed into her pockets and she looked as if she had been crying.

"Susan." Jonathan's voice acquired a sharpness and directness I would not have thought possible for him. I gave him a curious glance as he glared at the poor girl.

"I, I need to talk to you," she looked down at me, her eyes studying my face carefully before darting back to his, "about my grade, you know."

"Yes, I know." His tone softened a bit, but still sounded imperative, authoritative. "But my office hours are tomorrow." He pulled a small calendar out of his shirt pocket. "I'm free from one to three. You should come by then."

She was obviously too young to hear the finality in his voice. "But, it's important, and I thought that..."

"Tomorrow, Susan. From one to three."

She stood almost defiantly in front of us for a few final seconds, then her shoulders drooped and she walked to a booth further in the back of the diner. I watched her as she slid into her seat, her back to us. The other girl she was sitting with shook her head and from the expression on her face I got the impression she was scolding Susan. I wished I could read lips.

"Mara?" Jonathan's voice was apologetic now. "I'm sorry we were interrupted. Students just can't seem to get the idea that I'm not available twenty-four hours a day."

"She's very pretty." I didn't mean anything by the comment but that. Jonathan shifted in his seat uneasily.

"Yes, I suppose she is. But," he spoke faster than normal, "her grades are atrocious and her grasp of the material non-existent. I've been helping her as much as I could, giving her special tutoring, but she doesn't seem to get it." Then he shrugged and smiled. "We don't really need to discuss this, tonight, do we? I get enough of it during working hours."

"No," I said agreeably, "let's talk about something other than your job."

Even if he hadn't seemed relieved at my dismissal of the subject, I was glad to move on to other matters. I didn't know him well enough to want to get involved with his students or his academic career. What he did really made very little difference to me.

The server came by and took our dinner orders. After she left, Jonathan looked over at me. "How'd everything go today?"

"Fine, thanks. The movers were so late that I fell asleep waiting for them, but other than that..." My voice trailed away as I remembered the dream I'd had. The fragrance of the roses, the touch of those cold hands on me, the instant response of my body, the way I must have undressed myself in my sleep... Jesus, Mara, I thought, blushing furiously at the thought of how aroused I had been, how aroused even just the memory could make me, calm down. Don't work yourself into a sexual frenzy about some stupid dream.

"Mara? Come back, you're miles away."

I opened my eyes to Jonathan's face. His confusion was apparent, as was his concern.

"I'm sorry," I said, feeling confused myself. My stomach was tight, my heart racing and I began to tremble.

"Are you cold?" He stood up and took his jacket off. "Here," he said, moving quickly to my side of the booth, "put this on." In a chivalrous manner, he draped it over my shoulders and I pulled it tight around me.

"Thanks," I smiled and slid over on the seat as he sat down next to me. "I guess I did get a sort of chill. You really should do something about the heat up there."

"I'll check it tonight for you, if you want." His voice was warm and caressing and I gave him a sidelong glance, thinking that he was probably not much interested in the radiator, thinking, also, that an evening with him would probably be full of sexual revelations. But I'd resolved not to get involved with another man. And for some reason, the thoughts of his entering that apartment with me were frightening.

"Not tonight, Jonathan." My voice quavered just a bit and I cleared my throat. "But thanks anyway, maybe I could have a rain check."

"Sure thing. Anytime." His voice was calm and confident, as if he was unaware that I'd just turned him down. I glanced at him again. Maybe he was unaware, maybe it was just a friendly offer to help.

"So," I said, abruptly changing the subject, "what did you do today?"

"Now, we already agreed not to discuss my job. But how about you? Why don't you tell me about your paintings?"

I gave a small laugh. "No, that's no good, either. I don't really like to talk about what I do. Especially when I'm working on a project."

"Oh," his eyes lit with curiosity, "have you started painting already? What are you..." he caught himself mid-sentence and laughed. "Sorry. So what are we going to talk about?"

"Well," I said hesitantly, "I suppose we could talk about your ghost." Now what on earth possessed me to say that, I thought, there is no ghost.

"I'm not sure I've too much to say about him. Like I told you yesterday, no one has actually ever seen anything. Or if they have, they never told me about it."

"But you must have some idea who it is; I mean, you did say 'him' as if you knew the ghost was a man. And the house can't have had all that many owners, you should be able to narrow it down a bit."

"I thought you didn't believe in ghosts," he said.

"I don't. I was just trying to find something to talk about. And it's sort of fun to consider the possibility, don't you think? I've never lived in a haunted house before. It might be interesting."

"You're a weird one, Mara Hawthorne. I guess it must be your artistic temperament."

The server brought our food and Jonathan went to sit back opposite me. We ate silently for a while. The food was standard diner fare, but I'd never been particular about what I ate as long as someone else cooked it.

"Is your meal okay?"

"Great, thank you." I took one last bite and pushed my plate away.

"So tell me about yourself. Your parents, your childhood, why you decided to become an artist, things like that."

I gave a small, cynical laugh. "I don't think you ever decide to become an artist, as you put it. You're either one or you aren't; there's no middle ground." I shifted on my seat and leaned back into the corner of the booth. "My parents died when I was only five and I was shuffled around from foster home to foster home for the next thirteen years. Oh," I said quickly, trying to forestall the expressions of sympathy that usually followed my history, "it's not really as bad as it sounds. I barely remember my mom and dad; I have a few pictures and I know their names, but the memories just aren't there. And it was an interesting way to grow up, I suppose."

"Why weren't you ever adopted? You must have been a beautiful little girl."

I laughed. "Actually, nothing could be further from the truth. I was too skinny, too pale, too quiet, too placid..." I thought of all the other criticisms I'd endured over the years, "...well, you get the idea. I never matched up with anyone in particular; then one family, the MacIntyres, finally got tired of me scratching intricate designs into their furniture and drawing on their walls and sent me for art lessons. Things were easier after that, because I'd finally found something that I was good at. It didn't stop them from sending me on when my time was up, but, thank God, all the families I stayed with afterward kept up the classes. I can still hear the social worker telling each subsequent one, 'The art makes her easier to manage.'"

He reached over and held my hand briefly. "And so an artist was born."

"Yeah," I said and pulled my hand away from him, embarrassed that I'd told him so much. "So how about you? What was your family like?"

"Pretty normal, I guess."

The server brought our check and Jonathan paid it.

"It's bad enough that I dragged you away from your papers," I protested, "the least you can let me do is pay."

"Some other time," Jonathan got up and I followed him out of the diner.

On our walk home the wind began to gust, whipping wildly through the trees that lined the sidewalks.

"It'll rain tonight." He sounded so confident that I laughed.

"Oh, I see. Being a professor and a slumlord isn't enough. Now you want to be a weather man."

"Actually, you don't have to live here very long to make that prediction. It either rains or snows ten months out of the year in this town. And," he put his arms around me as we reached his front steps, "it's not cold enough tonight to snow."

In spite of my previous resolution, I responded eagerly when his mouth came down on mine. Jonathan Weber's kiss contradicted his shy, distracted manner. He was experienced—no question about that—he was very experienced and his hands sought out the exact places on my back and torso to stroke and touch. He pulled me closer into him and I could feel his arousal pressed hard against me. His lips were persistent, demanding and I wanted nothing more than to melt into his arms. But, I reminded myself with regret, I don't want a relationship, not here and not now, and I pushed away from him reluctantly. My breath came in soft pants as I shook my head.

"Rain check?" he asked, not angrily, but in a matter-of-fact tone, as if what he wanted were something as simple to give away as a cup of coffee. He smoothed an unruly strand of hair away from my face and his smile was so boyish, so seemingly innocent that I almost changed my mind.

A powerful gust of wind interrupted us and we both jumped at the loud crash behind us.

"What the hell?" he said, spinning around and staring at the shutter that had come loose in the wind and had fallen only a few feet behind him. "Damn," he turned back to me, a shocked expression erasing the passion from his face, "that could have hit us dead on."

My heart was pounding but I managed a shaky laugh. "I'll have to tell my landlord about this."

"Yeah," Jonathan said, laughing as well, "you do that."

"Anyway," I began, anxious suddenly to get upstairs, out of the brutal wind, "I had a nice time. Thank you."

"My pleasure, Mara." He moved toward me, but I backed away to the steps leading to the third floor.

"See you later, Jonathan."

"Oh, Mara," he called after me, "feel free to use the library up at the college. I'll sign for you."

"Thank you." I almost had to scream to be heard over the wind, but I didn't want to get any closer to him.

"What did you need to look up?"

God, doesn't he ever stop trying? "I need to look up some mythology. I could do it online..." I hesitated, not sure I could resist contacting the bad influences I was trying to escape. "Or I could just look at a copy of Bullfinch's mythology."

"What?" He came toward me and took my arm, guiding me to the steps. The side of the house provided some shelter from the wind, so I repeated my request as we walked up the stairs together.

"No problem," he replied, "I can easily find a copy of that downstairs. Come on back down..."

I interrupted him. "Thanks, tomorrow would be fine." I put my key into the door in a totally unsubtle hint, "I'd like to get some sleep now."

"Good night, Mara." Finally sensing my mood he made no further advances, but leaned toward me with a mischievous smile. "Oh, and Mara?"

"Yeah?"

"His name is probably Owen Culver."

"Whose name?" I couldn't follow his reasoning. Bullfinch's name was probably Owen Culver?

"The ghost. His name is Owen Culver." He turned away and hurried down the stairs. The rain began to pound on the roof as I entered my apartment, turning on the hall light and chuckling to myself at Jonathan's cleverness. He knew I would have to see him again to get the full story.

Still laughing, I shook my head as I locked the door. "Owen Culver, huh? But it won't work, Jonathan, I won't invite you in tonight to tell me about it." The rain continued to fall, heavier now and a flash of lightning lit the room brightly. When the flash was over, the room was in total darkness. "Great," I said, stumbling into the kitchen to find the candles I knew I had packed away somewhere, "just stinking great. My first night here and no lights."

The candles were, of course, in the very last box I chose to search. Finally, when I had them lit and set around the apartment, I'd enough light to find my way around, but not enough, I realized, to paint. I went back into the kitchen and pulled out a set of sheets and a blanket from the linens box and made the bed. Then I unpacked a few more of the cartons, stopping when I found a large plastic tumbler and the bottle of scotch. I went to the living room and curled up in my favorite armchair, drinking and watching the rain run down the studio windows.

It must have been quite a few hours later when I woke; the storm had calmed, my glass of scotch was on the floor and several of the candles had gone out, but at least the overhead light was back on. I stretched and got out of the chair, going to the lamp on my dresser and turning it on. Then I went back to the entryway and turned out the overhead switch. Blowing out the remaining candles, I stopped at the radiator and adjusted the knob again. A burst of warmed air hit me and I smiled, stripping off my clothes. I had been hoping that I would not have to wear anything to bed; I preferred to sleep the way I painted: in the nude. "Thank you," I whispered as I turned out the lamp, "and good night to you, Owen Culver, whoever the hell you are."

The scent of the candles I had extinguished followed me into my dreams and once again I was in a strange version of the apartment. The furniture was different, not the old pieces of junk I had brought, but beautifully restored antiques. Where the overhead light had been now hung a beautiful crystal chandelier, the flames of its candles dancing in the warm spring breeze, glass prisms sighing their tingling music through the room. Flowers, drooping with heavy blooms, flooded my senses with their warm, exotic scents. I sighed, it was all so beautiful, so much more fitting than before, and I felt as if I had finally, after all those long years, arrived home.

Wrapping the top sheet around my naked body, I sat up in bed, unmistakably my bed by the creaking and groaning of the springs. Everything else around me was different, except the canvas I had started that afternoon set up in the studio. I squinted at it across the room and saw that it, too, had changed; the figure of Apollo was more defined, more real, than I had painted. And Daphne looked more like me than I remembered.

How interesting, I thought, I must see it closer. But a warm languor overcame me and I was unable get out of bed. Instead, I settled back on the pillows and threw back the sheets. Looking down at my naked body, I compared it to the painting. Yes, she is very much like me, and I ran my hands along the contours of my breasts, my stomach, my upper thighs, as if through exploring my own body, I could gain a better understanding of hers. All the while, the eyes of Apollo seemed to fasten on me; eyes of flashing electric blue, watching my movements intently, hungrily.

I gasped. They were devouring eyes, inhuman eyes that I could never have painted, eyes that would have driven me away screaming if I were awake. *It's only a dream.* That thought relaxed me, because when I knew it was a dream, I was not afraid. The sensuality of his stare, the way his eyes lingered caressingly on my lips and breasts, and the promises those eyes held—days and nights of love and lust and unimaginable passion—intrigued me, aroused me, made me hot and desperate, oh God, so desperate for the touch of another pair of hands.

I should have invited Jonathan in, I thought, as my body writhed and my back arched in invitation to anyone that could ease the teasing torment. There could be no easing, since no one was there.

"I don't want to be alone," I half groaned the words. "I want someone, anyone, I don't care who."

As if my words had weight to touch the air around me, the chandelier rocked back and forth, several of the candles blew out and the prisms jangled discordantly. In the flickering light, the figure that had been watching me from the painting seemed to move, the outlines wavered as if a veil had passed over them, or had fallen away. I should be frightened, I thought, I should call for help, but my voice froze in my throat, and the hot, sensual languor still held control of my body. I licked my lips as I stared at the wispy outline of the man and my breath came in soft, short gasps. "You're only a dream," I breathed to him over the scented air, "but I don't care. I want you, come to me."

The touch on my foot was barely perceptible at first, except as an easing, a cooling for my blazing flesh. I sighed and closed my eyes, savoring the sensation. Cold fingers crawled up my ankle, slowly caressed the skin of my knees, and lingered there, teasing and tantalizing.

"Mara," the whispering of my name thrilled my entire body, "Mara."

The cool touch of his breath on my skin caused me to cry out in incoherent longing. The ghostly fingers seemed warmer as if the fire of my flesh had given them life, and they traveled further up my legs, kneading my thighs. And when they finally reached and thrust deeply into the center of my body's heat, I was completely lost, beyond knowing this for a dream, beyond caring who or what he was.

"Ah," I breathed, "so good, so good, never wake up..."

I was answered only by a deeper probing and an almost imperceptible laugh. I bit my lip and thrashed about on the bed, giving small moans and grunts until the orgasm rocked me, screaming and panting.

I gave one final shudder and fell back, out of breath and sweating profusely. The bed creaked again, and the mattress shifted, as if someone were moving next to me. When I reached over, though, there was nothing to feel.

"Don't go away," I begged the emptiness, "come back and let me see you, let me touch you."

"I will be back, Mara," he whispered, his deep echoing voice caused delicious chills to wash over me, "you will see and touch me soon. And I will leave you a gift, so you never need go to anyone else."

Then there was silence and I felt his departure as if it were physical pain. "No," I called to him, struggling to open my eyes, trying to reach out to him so that he wouldn't leave, "I don't want a gift. I want you. Don't go."

A loud thump in the hallway and the sound of a door closing somewhere woke me with a start. I opened my eyes to the sun that was streaming in through the studio windows and I could see that the painting was exactly as I had left it the previous afternoon. Apollo had no eyes, and only the mere suggestion of a body. "God," I said stretching and pulling myself out of bed, "that was really weird." Wrapping the sweat-soaked top sheet around me, I went down the stairs to see what had fallen to wake me up.

Directly inside the front door was a book and I bent down to pick it up. It was a copy of Bullfinch's *The Age of Fable*, an old book, but in perfect condition, beautifully bound in black leather with gold leaf titles. I carried it up the stairs and sat down in an armchair to look at it closer.

Opening the cover, I was surprised to discover that it was a first edition, more surprised still to see my name inscribed on the flyleaf. "To Mara Hawthorne," it read, "a woman belonging to a different age." There was no signature, but I knew the only person who could have given it to me was Jonathan Weber. He was also, curiously enough, the only person who could have unlocked my front door. I felt flattered at the value of the book and his generosity. I laughed to myself. *What the hell would he have given me if I had slept with him?* Then again, at the same time, I was annoyed that he felt free enough to enter my apartment without my permission.

"So," I said, opening the first page and beginning to read, "I'll just let him stew a while before I thank him."

It was well after twelve when I closed the book. My stomach was empty and hollow; I realized that I hadn't eaten since last night. Not only that, I hadn't been grocery shopping since I arrived and there was no food in the apartment. When I got up from the chair, I realized how exhausted I was. The bed, even disheveled as it was, looked so very tempting. What I really needed was a nice, long nap, but I forced myself to get dressed and go out.

When I went outside, I saw that it was raining lightly. That, plus the difficulties of carrying bags of groceries back with me, made me decide to take my car, even though the closest food store was only a few blocks away. Stopping at the bank first, I opened a local account and ordered a debit card and a set of checks. When I finally made it to the food store it was around one-thirty. Pushing the cart down the aisles half-heartedly, I finally picked up enough to keep me going for at least a month. Although I did buy some fresh fruit and vegetables, most of the food I bought was junk: pre-prepared meals, frozen dinners, and microwave entrees for one. I'd never been much of a cook and when I was painting I liked something quick and easy.

The cashier was, I thought, overly friendly, a buxom, middle-aged brown-haired woman who liked to talk. Unfortunately, I'd always had a certain waif-like quality that seemed to bring out the worst in these matronly types. But I smiled and made the appropriate responses to her questions, because the name on her tag was the same as my mother's.

"You're new around here, aren't you, honey?"

"Yes," I admitted, "I just moved in yesterday."

"Not a student, are you?" She gave me a long appraising glance, then shook her head without giving me a chance to respond. "Nope, you don't look like a student. Where are you staying?"

"I have a third floor apartment over on Pine Street."

Her hand seemed to hesitate over the price reader. "Not the Weber house, is it?" It seemed ridiculous, but her voice sounded pitched higher as she said it.

I nodded, "Yes, it's very nice. Jonathan has just redecorated the place. Has he owned it long?"

"Been in his family ever since I can remember. It was his idea to turn it into apartments, though. Said it was too big for a bachelor." She bagged and totaled my order and I handed her cash.

She chuckled. "We don't see much of the green stuff these days. We do take credit if you'd prefer."

"Nope, cash is good with me." I'd had to cancel all my accounts to keep them safe from my ex's attentions. "I just opened my bank account and don't have my checks or my debit card yet."

She nodded. "In that case would you like to fill out a check-cashing card for next time, honey?" She opened the cash register drawer and counted out my change. "That makes it easier for you than carrying around a lot of money."

I didn't really care, but she seemed so eager to help that I agreed. "That would be nice, thank you."

She turned the key in her register. "I'll just pick one up for you over at the office. Be back in a sec."

I spent the time studying the stand of papers next to me. I laughed at some of the stories covered, especially the one about the alien advising the president. Damn, I thought, vampires, alien invasions, half-wolf babies, haunted houses—people will believe almost anything.

"You want one of those, honey?" The cashier's voice brought me out of my thoughts, "I can add it on, if you like."

"No," I said with a half-grin, "but I'll take a local paper if you have one."

She pulled one off the stack at the end of her register and placed it on top of the filled bags in my cart. "That'll be fifty cents and here's the form for the card. Why don't you fill it out now, since we aren't busy and you can pay by check next time you stop."

I handed her two quarters from the change she'd given me earlier and started to fill out the card. She leaned over the counter, watching me intently. "You live alone?"

I was beginning to get annoyed at her prying. "Well, unless you count Owen Culver as company, I guess I do."

This time there was no questioning her reaction. She stiffened slightly, looked around almost guiltily, and gave a small nervous laugh. "Owen Culver?" She whispered the name as if it were an obscenity. "I haven't heard that name in years. Have you seen him?"

"No, I haven't seen him. I was only joking." I handed her the paper. "Thank you. I guess I'll be seeing you around."

I started to push the cart out the door when I felt a hand on my shoulder. "Mara," she must have read my name on the form. Her voice was low and earnest, and she followed me out to my car, lightly putting her hand on my arm. "Owen Culver is nothing to joke about. Tell that Jonathan Weber you want out of your lease and move somewhere else. A little thing like you, all on your own, in that house, why, honey, it just gives me the chills. Move out."

I didn't say anything, but shut the lid of the trunk on the groceries I had been unloading while she talked. My stomach rolled;

I was tired, hungry and in no mood to argue with a total stranger about my choice of living quarters. "Thank you again," I said, a note of finality in my voice, and put the car keys into my purse. "I'll think about it."

"Well then, you take care," she called after me. I crossed the street and approached the pizza place Jonathan had pointed out last night. Before I entered I looked back and the cashier was still standing there staring after me. In spite of the fact that I felt slightly nauseous and my legs were wobbly, I gave her a bright smile and waved. She nodded her head. "Remember what I told you," she called to me and went back into the store.

I went into the pizza parlor grinning to myself. People will believe anything.

The place was empty, although used plates and napkins were strewn about several of the tables. Checking my watch I realized that it was too late for lunch and too early for dinner. I stood waiting for a few minutes and when no one appeared to take my order, I rang the bell on the counter.

"Be right there," a young female voice called out from the back, and the girl who had spoken to Jonathan last night in the diner walked out. She seemed less weepy today and although I could tell she recognized me, she didn't smile. In fact, she came as close to not acknowledging my presence as was possible in the situation.

"Hi," I said, "Susan, isn't it?"

"Yeah," she said sullenly, "what do you want?"

I looked up at the menu, "I'll have a small, with extra cheese, bacon, pepperoni, and green peppers. And a large cola."

She rang up my food and when I paid, she pointed to the seating area. "Take a booth; I'll bring it out when it's ready."

I chose the cleanest table and sat down. A radio was playing in the back of the store and I closed my eyes, lightly tapping my fingers to the song's rhythm. I was so tired; my head drooped and I pulled it back, attempting to shake off the strange exhaustion that overcame me.

The next thing I knew, a teenaged boy I hadn't seen before set my pizza and drink on the table.

"You okay, lady?"

"Yeah," I said, rubbing my forehead and eyes, "I guess I just nodded off. Where's Susan?"

"She had an appointment," he shrugged, "You want anything else?"

"No, this'll be fine, thanks."

Eating revived my energy slightly and I managed to finish all but one piece of pizza. After drinking the soda, I felt awake enough for the drive back home. I thought about taking the last piece home for later, but when I stood up I felt as if I was going to be sick. I threw a few dollars on the table for a tip and rushed out.

By the time I crossed the street to my car the wave of nausea passed. Nevertheless, I drove home with the window open. The cool rain on my face made me feel clean and refreshed, but when I arrived at my apartment, I was soaked and chilled. I swore as I got out of the car realizing I still had to get six bags of groceries up the stairs and put them away. And I was so tired.

"Jesus," I said, balancing two bags of frozen food, turning the key in my lock and kicking the door open, "it's not as if I didn't sleep last night. This is crazy." I dumped the bags on the landing and went back down for another load.

The rest of the bags were too heavy to carry more than one at a time. Finally, after what seemed countless trips up and down the stairs, I dragged the last bag from the trunk and slammed the lid down. A car pulled up behind me and honked its horn. I spun around and the bag broke open, spilling cans and bottles onto the sidewalk.

"Shit," I looked at the mess at my feet, leaned up against my car, and began to cry.

Jonathan Weber was out of his car in a second, wrapping an arm around my shoulders, and apologizing. "Oh, God, Mara, I'm so sorry, I didn't think you'd drop it."

"I didn't drop it," I squeezed the words out between sobs, "the goddamned thing broke."

He patted my shoulder, "Are you crying?"

I choked a bit and nodded my head.

"Aw, don't cry, Mara, I'll collect it all for you and bring it up. You're sopping wet, you go on and get dry, and I'll be along in a minute."

"Thank you." I dragged myself up the stairs for what I hoped would be the last time that day. I tripped over the bags that I'd left on the landing, swore again, and went into the bathroom. Leaving my clothes in a sodden heap in the tub, I wrapped myself in a towel, and walked out of the bathroom, just as Jonathan came in the front door.

He stopped and stared at me for a minute before averting his eyes. "I'm sorry again," he said, the expression I had caught in his eyes indicated he was anything but sorry to catch me practically naked. "You go change and I'll put some of this stuff away for you."

"Fine," I said, in a tone more biting than I intended, "just come on in and make yourself at home." Then I stalked over to the bedroom alcove and pulled the curtains. The bed was even more inviting than it'd been before I left and I wanted nothing more than to crawl into it and pull the covers over my head. "But no," I said quietly, nastily, "now I have to entertain my landlord."

"Did you say something?" Jonathan called.

"No, not really." I knew none of this was Jonathan's fault, he was actually trying to help, so I made an effort to respond cheerfully. "Oh, Jonathan, put the kettle on while you're at it and we'll have a cup of tea or something after I'm dressed."

"Good idea." Jonathan's voice was enthusiastic, eager.

I smiled to myself, while I pulled a pair of jeans and a sweater from my dresser. It's likely he's more interested in the 'or something' than the tea, Mara, so you go easy. As I started to slide the jeans up my legs, I noticed that the skin on my legs and thighs was discolored with angry looking red streaks. I sat down on the bed and touched the marks tentatively. The skin wasn't broken and the marks weren't painful. Shaking my head, I rubbed my legs once more, then lay back on the bed and stared at the ceiling...

"Mara? Are you okay?" Jonathan's voice woke me and I sat up quickly.

"Fine," I called and got up from the bed and finished dressing.

Sliding out from behind the curtains, I went to the bathroom and picked up a dry towel. "You sure were right about the rain," I admitted as I walked into the kitchen, rubbing my wet hair. "Do you think it will stop soon?"

I wondered how long I had been asleep. There was no sign of the groceries I'd bought and I assumed Jonathan had put them away for me. Now he was standing at the sink, washing some fruit. He chuckled and made a show of looking at the clock. "Oh, it'll probably stop in about three or four weeks. We're in the rain belt, you know."

"Oh." I sat down at the kitchen table and watched him for a while. He found a bowl and put the fruit into it, then sat it down in front of me.

"Here," he said graciously, as if we were in his apartment instead of mine, "have something to eat. You'll feel better. The water should be hot, soon." He went over to the stove and shook the kettle. "Here we go," he said as it whistled, "just what the doctor ordered." He filled the two mugs he had prepared and put them on the table along with two spoons, the sugar bowl, and a small container of milk.

I dipped the tea bag up and down, distractedly. "You know, Jonathan," I said as he sat down across from me, "you don't need to wait on me. I can take care of myself."

"Yeah," he said, "I'm sure you can. But you just looked so down, so tired, I thought I should help you out a bit."

"Well," I poured some milk into my tea and took a sip, "thank you. I appreciate it. Just don't..." Don't make a habit of it was what I wanted to say, but he looked so sincere, so boyish, that I softened the thought. "Just don't spoil me too much."

"So, how'd you sleep last night?"

"What?"

"You know, with the storm and all. Did you lay awake all night listening to the rain?"

"No," I felt a slow blush creep up my neck, recalling the dream, "I slept great. I don't even remember hearing the rain."

"That's good. I see you were even prepared for the electricity going out," he waved an arm around, "all these candles. You were better off than I was, I just stumbled around, cursing the darkness."

"You should've called," I said without thinking, "I would've given you some." I blushed again, realizing that, given our circumstances last night, what I said was a double-entendre. "You know, candles."

He had the good grace not to refer to my slip. "I might have done that, but the phones were out too. And, you gave me the distinct impression you wanted to be alone."

"Well," I said with a tired smile, "there's that."

An uncomfortable silence fell over us. I sipped my tea and closed my eyes to think. Now was probably the time to thank him for the book, but I still resented his intrusion and didn't want him to get the idea he could walk in at any time. I came here to paint, I reminded myself again, not to carry on an affair with my landlord.

"Well," Jonathan's voice sounded slightly harsh interposed on the quiet sound of the rain hitting the roof, "aren't you even going to ask?"

I lifted my head up and opened my eyes with great effort. I had almost nodded off again. "Ask about what?"

"Owen Culver."

"Oh," I said with a small laugh, "him again. He's getting to be quite the topic of conversation."

"Why? Who have you been talking to?" Jonathan seemed angry that I might've heard the story from someone else.

I laughed again. "The cashier in the grocery store, for one. Although she didn't really have much to say about him, she just told me to break my lease and move out. But she did give me the feeling that I might as well move in with Satan himself as live here. What was he, anyway? Some sort of ax murderer?"

"Owen? God, no, he was nothing that horrible. For a man of his time, I suspect he was quite a hell-raiser, but in a totally different way. According to all reports, he was a heartless philanderer."

I chuckled as I got up and put the heat under the tea kettle again. "And for that he's doomed to haunt my apartment forever? Seems to me he's gotten a bad rap. Although," I took an apple from the bowl and bit into it, leaning back on the counter, "considering my luck with men, it figures I would move into the situation."

"Your luck with men—why should you say that?" Jonathan's voice was sharp, offended.

I gave him a quick glance, "I have a notorious habit of picking the worst possible partner. But I don't really want to discuss any of that. So what happened to Owen Culver that he should still be around?"

"Well," Jonathan lowered his voice slightly and looked around, "he was murdered."

"Really?" I had a feeling I knew what Jonathan was leading up to and surprisingly it didn't bother me. But I played the game as expected. "Where?"

"I don't want to alarm you, but they found his body here, over in your studio. The father of a girl he had gotten pregnant shot him twice, once in the heart, and once in the genitals. They say it took years to get the blood stain out of the floor, and that every year on the anniversary of his death it comes back."

I tried to put the proper expression of fear and loathing on my face but didn't quite succeed. Finally, much to Jonathan's surprise, I burst out in hysterical laughter. The harder I tried to control my reaction, the funnier the situation seemed. Tears streamed down my face and my stomach started to ache.

"It's true," he said indignantly. I could tell that he didn't know how to respond, that my laughter really threw him off balance. "And I don't see what's so funny. Owen Culver was my great-great-grandmother's brother, and I swear this is all true."

"And now I'm supposed to swoon into your arms in fear, right?" I smirked at him, not unkindly, then chuckled and shook my head. "So tell me, Jonathan, does this story usually work for you?"

"Well," he gave me the innocent, boyish smile of his that I found so endearing, "it doesn't hurt most of the time. Not going to buy it, are you?"

"No, not this time. No offense, okay?"

"Okay. But tell me the truth, aren't you even the slightest bit frightened, knowing the awful facts of Uncle Owen?"

"Jesus, Jonathan, I lived ten years in New York and not always in the best of areas. People got shot all the time, although," and I giggled again irreverently, "not always in such an appropriate spot. Poor Owen, I said before he'd gotten a bad rap and now I know it's true. Knowing the truth, as you put it, doesn't frighten me. If anything, it's probably made me more sympathetic toward him." The teakettle whistled and I filled my cup again. "That is, it would if I believed in him. So, when's his anniversary? I'll look out for the stain and call the papers if it appears."

Jonathan gave me an odd look, and I got the impression that he was more spooked than he let on. "Actually, it's in two weeks. You might want to arrange to be somewhere else at the time. You know, just in case."

I smiled at him. "Your place, for instance?"

Jonathan shrugged, "Well, you'd be more than welcome, then or any other time, for that matter."

"I'll be sure to remember that," I said dryly.

He got up from the table and stood in front of me. "I guess I'd better be going, then. I still have a stack of papers to grade from the other night." Awkwardly, he bent toward me to give me a kiss.

His lips never made it to mine. A crash from the studio made him jump and turn around. "What the hell was that?"

The canvases that I had stacked in the corner had fallen over, narrowly missing my current painting. I walked over and set them upright again. "You know, Jonathan, if you're so jumpy about this place, you probably shouldn't be telling ghost stories."

"It's not that," he said sharply, "the noise startled me, that's all." He moved across the room and looked at the canvas I had started. "Is this your new one?"

I nodded, slightly embarrassed. I didn't like people evaluating my work until it was completed, if then. Suddenly, inexplicably angry, I stood with my arms crossed, as if daring him to make a comment, any comment, while we both studied the painting.

"Daphne and Apollo," was all he said. Then his lips brushed my cheek delicately. "I'll see you later, I hope." He was halfway down the stairs when I pulled my attention from the unfinished canvas long enough to realize that he'd left.

"Yeah," I called to him, not taking my gaze from the nebulous figures that danced in front of me, pleading with imagined eyes and hands for the life my paint would impart, "later." Before the front door had even closed, I was taking off my sweater, my jeans, and pulling a brush out of the can. Thoughts of Jonathan Weber and Owen Culver, of erotic dreams and philandering ghosts, faded into nothing as the work completely possessed my mind.

By six o'clock the next morning I had done as much painting as was physically possible for me at one time. I'd been at it for over fourteen hours; my legs ached, my arms trembled and my spine felt as if it had been tied into a thousand knots. But none of that mattered since the figures of Apollo and Daphne had been given life and form.

The smooth skin of Daphne's thighs and stomach was overlaid with the rough gnarls of bark, her wind-blown hair becoming tendrils, green and growing, her outstretched arms sprouting the stubs of limbs and branches. Small beads of sap and blood and sweat dappled her virginal breasts; the exhilaration of the chase seemed to drain from her face as she realized the fate to which she had condemned herself. A slight twist to her mouth suggested that perhaps she now regretted her hasty prayer for salvation.

"Too late, babe," I addressed her, my hands on my hips, "Didn't anyone ever tell you that it's better to be a ravished nymph than a virgin tree? Anyway," my gaze now went to the figure of Apollo, "how could you resist him?"

Even to my usually self-critical eyes, the Apollo was magnificent. He had come up behind her, catching her by the tiny waist, twisting her around to accept his embrace. From one hand fluttered the garment he had ripped from the nymph's body, the other hand grasped the skin soon to be bark with long, sensuous fingers. The muscles of his chest glistened with sweat and his face glowed with passion. He was completely naked and his penis was startlingly erect.

I shivered; the portrayal of Daphne was good, I knew, as good or perhaps slightly better than most of my paintings. But the figure of Apollo frightened me, he was so shockingly lifelike. I ached to put my hand on his chest, to draw him to me, to fall with him to the forest floor and make love there beneath the branches of the woman who'd denied him.

"She didn't love you," I said with only half a smile for my foolishness, "but I do. I would stay with you forever."

I stood, swaying in front of the canvas for a long time, caught up in the spell of the story and the spell of his eyes. Have you come from my brush or from the longings of my soul? I could hardly remember painting him; he seemed the culmination of my dreams, not just the ones I'd experienced here, but all my dreams and fantasies. If only you were real, I thought and felt tears of despair streaming down my face.

The sound of a toilet flushing in the apartment downstairs finally brought me back to reality with a start. I shook myself and went into the shower, wiping my eyes and laughing. "Jesus, Mara, you've been working too long."

After I'd dried off, I realized that I was too keyed up to sleep; the exhaustion of the day before was gone in face of the exhilaration of my creation. I dressed in my last pair of clean jeans and an oversized t-shirt, rummaged through the closet for my raincoat, picked up my keys and went down the stairs.

The morning sun was pale and shrouded with clouds, but the air was clean. I felt that I could almost see the growth of the grass and the early spring flowers bursting through the sodden earth. Walking slowly as if in a trance, I went around the block, touching each tree I saw in a ritual homage.

I passed Jonathan's porch and headed for my side stairway, when I heard my name called and turned around. He was sitting on a chair, his feet propped up on the railing next to a steaming mug. He folded the paper he'd been reading, dropped it on the porch, and stood up.

"Good morning, Mara. You're up early, aren't you? I thought you artists slept late."

He hadn't shaved, and the flannel shirt he wore was unbuttoned. I stared at him as if I'd never seen him before and suddenly realized that Jonathan bore an arresting resemblance to my Apollo. Maybe it was the set of his jaw, the musculature of his chest, or just the way his eyes looked at me, with passion and promise. Whatever it was, I wanted to throw myself onto him and rip the clothes from his body to see if the rest of him matched the god who waited for me upstairs. Instead, I put my hands into my pockets and blushed.

"Actually," I said quietly, not daring to move, "I haven't been to bed. Yet." The last word lingered in the air like an invitation.

"Well then," he said with a broad smile, his teeth flashing white against his unshaven face, "maybe you'd like to come in for a cup of coffee."

I nodded, not trusting my voice. He came down the few steps and wrapped his arm around my waist, pulling me to him.

Once we were inside, he shut the door and locked it. I could feel the click of the latch deep within me and my pulse raced. Jonathan reached over and took my hands in his, smiling down into my face. "You really didn't come here for coffee, did you?"

I wanted to insist that I did, but my trembling hands betrayed me. "No," I admitted, my voice a frightened whisper, "I came for you."

"That's what I hoped."

Jonathan didn't waste any time; he scooped me up, carried me back to his bedroom and gently deposited me onto his enormous bed. It was still unmade, and the covers were thrown back to reveal black satin sheets. It did not seem like a bed designed for sleep, it was designed instead for seduction. He loomed over me, the smile I'd found so charming now seemed merely arrogant and the hands that removed my jeans and my panties were so expert, so practiced that I began to doubt that this was what I really wanted.

But at least he's real, Mara, I thought, my eyes darting about trying to focus on anything but his face, and his now naked body, *he's not a dream or a dead god on canvas. He's live and tangible and here.* The thought reassured me and I gave him a quavering smile as he removed my shirt. Soon I lay naked in front of him.

"Mara," he said, but the voice was not the one I wanted to hear, "I feel like I've known you forever, like I've waited forever for you." He lay down next to me, his hands busy, touching and stroking my breasts. His mouth nibbled at my neck, murmuring endearments, urging me to relax, to let him love me. My body responded to him fully, but my mind was somewhere else. And although I tried to ignore where it took me, I knew the location with certainty: two flights up in a fragrant bower that existed only in my imagination.

When Jonathan finally entered me, I made the appropriate responses, my moans and cries joining his, my traitor body moving to his thrusts and pounding. He ducked his head to suck at my nipples, saying my name over and over and I arched my back to meet him. He began to grunt, screaming his pleasure, his release and his frenzied pulsing brought me quickly to orgasm.

He rolled from me with a sigh that I echoed and he misunderstood. "Yeah," he said, reaching for a tissue to remove the condom I hadn't even realized he'd used, "I agree, that was incredible." He kissed me on the forehead then sat up. "But unfortunately, I have a class in about," he looked at a bedside clock, "oh, forty-five minutes, so I have to go." I turned my head and sighed again, feeling tears well up in my eyes. Jonathan did not notice, instead he left the room and went straight to the shower.

By the time he returned, I'd gotten control of my emotions and my disappointment. *Of course it was nothing like your dreams, you silly girl,* I thought scathingly, *what on earth could be?* Two weeks ago I would've been ecstatic over the sex. Jonathan was a good lover, an interesting person and he seemed to be crazy about me. There was absolutely no reason for me to be disappointed.

I watched him furtively as he dressed; he had a nice body, not as muscular nor as massive as the painting, but certainly nothing to be ashamed of. When he finished tying his tie and selecting a suit coat, he came over and sat next to me on the bed, giving the side of my hip a gentle slap.

"I'm so sorry I have to rush away, but why don't you just stay here and get some sleep? Make yourself at home; have some coffee or breakfast or whatever. And remember," he smiled and brushed back my hair where it had fallen, partially covering my breasts, "that I won't mind at all if you're still here when I get back."

I listened to his footsteps until the front door closed. Then I pulled the black satin sheet over me, rolled to my side and fell fast asleep.

When I woke, I was confused to hear Jonathan speaking. I knew he'd left and hadn't heard the door open, so he couldn't be back. I pulled on my t-shirt and followed the sound of his voice. When I got to the kitchen, I understood as I heard, "So if you'll leave your name, your number and a brief message, I'll call you right back."

I laughed, poured myself a cup of coffee and went to turn the volume down on his machine. Although he'd invited me and obviously wanted me to stay, that didn't entitle me to listen in on his messages. But the urgency of the caller's voice stopped my hand and I sat down at the kitchen table with a flop when I recognized her voice.

"Hi, uh, Jonathan, it's me." It was Susan, the girl from the diner and the pizza place. "I took the test this morning and it was positive." She paused and I could hear the tears in her voice. "And you know how you said last night that you would take care of me, if I were, well, you know." She blew her nose and continued, "Well, I am." A long pause ensued. "Oh, God, Jonathan, I'm pregnant." After finally breaking the bad news her words began to flow so fast I almost had difficulty following them.

"And you know it's yours, there's never been anyone else, and I love you and you said last night that you loved me and that you would take care of me. And last night was so wonderful, you know, and I'm sorry I was so mad about you being out with that woman, I know you don't like her, she's too old for you, that's what you said and you just took her out to dinner because you felt sorry that she was all alone. And, well anyway, I wanted you to know that I do understand and I feel better and I know you'll take care of me. Call me when you get home and I can come over again tonight." Susan paused again, then repeated in a plaintive voice, "I love you. Call me."

I sat quietly for a few seconds listening to the tape on the answering machine click back into place. I took a sip of the coffee, it was too strong, too bitter. Flinging the mug as hard as I could, I delighted in the crashing of the pieces as they shattered and fell down to the floor beneath the phone.

That goddamned son of a bitch. I kept repeating it over and over as I dressed. *That goddamned son of a bitch.* "Waited forever for me, huh?" I addressed his bed as if it were him, "'And last night was so wonderful,'" I mimicked, "Jesus, Jonathan, last night? Your bed hardly even cooled off from Susan before you eased me into it." *That goddamned son of a bitch.* "Well, since this 'woman' is too old for you, someone you just feel sorry for, I can promise you it'll be a cold day in hell before I get in here with you again." Angrily, I ripped the black satin sheets completely off the bed, rolled them up into a crumpled ball, and threw them into the corner of the room.

That goddamned son of a bitch.

I slammed his front door and stormed up the stairs to my apartment, taking my shoes off and kicking them clear across the room. I stopped in front of my canvas just long enough to throw a drop cloth over it, "And I don't need you looking at me again while I'm sleeping. You're the one that got me into this in the first place; standing there so goddamned sexy, making me want someone, looking just enough like him to make it happen."

I crawled into bed, still ranting at the covered painting, knowing that eventually my anger would run its course and I would be fine. "You're all the same, every stinking one of you, you can't keep your dicks inside your pants long enough to stay out of trouble. Even poor Owen couldn't keep his hands off the ladies to save his life. I swear if I had a gun, I'd shoot the genitals off every man I meet, before they can hurt me." With that last vindictive statement my rage ran out; I wiped the tears from my face, pulled the covers up over my still clothed body and fell asleep.

I slept until late that afternoon, dreamlessly. Maybe my anger kept the erotic dreams away, maybe since I'd just had a living man my subconscious decided that I didn't need a dream lover, or maybe just covering the painting removed the influence on my overly active imagination. Whatever the reason, the undisturbed rest was exactly what I needed, and when I woke up I felt revitalized, able to look at the situation with Jonathan in a different light.

I remembered my anger of this morning almost sheepishly. It wasn't as if Jonathan had pledged his eternal love to me. It wasn't as if we meant anything more to each other than just plain sex. No promises had been made between us, it was not my trust he had betrayed. I felt more sorry for Susan now than I did for myself. "But now's as good a time as any, sweetie, to learn how the world works. That's what college is for."

I showered to wash Jonathan's touch from my body. There was still anger, I realized, but now I knew that most of it was directed at myself for allowing this to happen. "Never again," I said as I got out of the shower and looked at my reflection in the mirror. "Never again." I brushed my teeth, dried my hair and dressed in the jeans I had worn that morning, but dropped my t-shirt in the hamper.

Putting my hand to the knob of the bathroom door, I gave a self-depreciating laugh, "So how about it, Owen? From now on it'll just be you and me, two lost souls together." I snorted, "After all, love's never done much for either of us, has it?"

When I opened the door, I was unprepared for the blast of cold air that met me. I shivered and went to the radiator, adjusting the knob, but nothing happened. "Dammit," I swore, "I need some heat. It's as cold as a stinking tomb in here." I crossed my arms over my naked chest. "Come on, baby," I urged the radiator, "give your friend Mara a little heat." It sighed and sputtered and gave off one more gush of cold before the heat filtered through. "Thank you."

I went to the closet and found one of my painting shirts still clean; buttoning it up, I thought that tomorrow I would have to find a laundromat. "But that's tomorrow," I went into the kitchen and pulled a prepared dinner from the freezer, "we still have to get through tonight."

When I'd finished the meal, I dumped the tray into the wastebasket and put my fork into the sink. I didn't feel much like painting, didn't own a television, didn't know anyone to call on the phone. It promised to be a long evening. I heard an odd fluttering outside my front door, but when I looked out the studio window, I saw that the wind was blowing hard again and more rain had started.

I went back to the kitchen and poured myself a large glass of scotch, tuned my clock radio to the college station and sat back in an armchair. "Well, Owen," I realized that talking to a non-existent ghost was probably worse than talking to yourself, but what the hell,

I was an artist and entitled to my eccentricities, "what's on the agenda for tonight? Maybe we should just sit around here and tell each other the dismal stories of our love lives." I refilled my glass and wandered about the apartment, ending up at the radiator, giving the knob one more twist.

"Ahhraa," it moaned at me.

"Not much of a conversationalist, are you?" I laughed, slightly drunk. "God, this is boring; I wish something would happen, I don't care what."

As I spoke, three things happened simultaneously. Lightning flashed, the lights went out and there was someone pounding on my front door. "Hold on a minute," I called to the person at the door, "my lights just went out." I lit one of the candles I'd used the previous night and walked down the stairs, opening the door to a wet and bedraggled Jonathan Weber. He gave me a twisted, sheepish grin, and extended his fist to me, offering about a dozen wilted roses in his fist.

"Hi," his voice was uncertain, "can I come in?"

"I don't think so," I said sternly.

"Just to talk, please."

"I can't think what we'd have to talk about, Jonathan. What happened this morning was a mistake from the beginning. I don't intend for it ever to happen again."

"I won't try anything, I promise," he smiled at me, his face seemed so sincere, so innocent, "I just want to explain. I think I have to explain."

"And that's an admirable sentiment, Jonathan. But you don't owe me an explanation. Just go home."

I tried to slam the door on his face, but he blocked the door with his body and pushed his way through. Closing the door behind him, he dropped the roses onto the floor of the landing and reached out to grab my shoulders. "Please, Mara, at least talk to me. I'll only stay a few minutes, I promise."

"Okay, but take your hands off me."

He let my shoulders go reluctantly and I darted up the steps before him. I went into the kitchen, put the candle on the table, and set my hand-wound timer.

"What's that for?" Jonathan stood before me, offering the roses again.

"I give you fifteen minutes. You can have your say and then leave." I took the roses from him and put them into the sink. "These won't help you any, either. I'm not that much of an old-fashioned girl to swoon away at the sight of a dozen long-stemmed roses."

"But I just found them outside your door. I didn't buy them intending to..."

"Like hell you didn't." I crossed my arms in front of me and leaned back on the counter. "So, talk," I said, tapping my finger on the timer dial, "your time is running out."

Jonathan took a big gulp of air. "I wanted to explain about Susan. I know you must've heard her message." He laughed uneasily, "I found the remains of your coffee cup on the floor."

I didn't say a word. The ticking of the timer was almost deafening in the silence and the near darkness.

"Well, I'll admit that Susan and I had a brief affair, and she sort of latched on to me. I've tried to break it off many times, but she always comes back. This isn't the first time she's thought she was pregnant, it probably won't be the last. For her, that is, but not for me. I talked to her today and told her that we're through. I promise you. If she really is pregnant, well then I'll help her out the best I can. But I don't love her, I love you."

I stared at him for a long minute. "How convenient for you that fathers today don't carry shotguns; otherwise you might end up like your great uncle Owen."

The apartment seemed to grow colder and Jonathan shifted nervously on his feet. "That's not funny, Mara."

"It wasn't meant to be, Jonathan. Does philandering run in the family, or do you just feel it to be a male prerogative?"

"Please, Mara, don't be like this." His voice was low and persuasive and he managed to sound totally sincere. "I want to make it up to you and I will. This morning was special to me, you have to believe that, and if I'd been able to stay I would have told you all about Susan." He hung his head slightly. "I'm not proud of any of this, but I love you. Hell, I'm not perfect, no one is, but I'd like a second chance with you. Please."

He couldn't have seen my expression soften in the candlelight, but he must have felt it. The cold air between us felt almost electric, and when his arms came around me I leaned into him.

"One second chance," I said sternly. "One. That's all you'll get from me."

He kissed me. I shivered. Standing here in the darkness with the scent of the roses in the sink seemed so close to my dreams. But I could feel him, could touch him and I knew that he wouldn't vanish when I woke.

Jonathan lifted me up on the counter and struggled with my buttons. When he couldn't undo them fast enough, he swore and ripped the entire shirt open, his mouth fastening hungrily to my breast.

I jumped and pushed his head away from me, "Jesus, do you have to be so rough?"

He looked up at me and his face seemed brutal in the candlelight. "I want you so bad, Mara. I have to have you, right here, right now."

"And if I say no?" My voice trembled, his passion was frightening, overwhelming and I didn't want to be swept up in it.

"Then," he said, his hand closing tightly over the crotch of my jeans, "I'll take you anyway. You know you want me, just say it, say you want me, Mara."

He worked my zipper down and pulled my jeans and panties down to my knees, fumbling with his own pants and dropping them to the floor. He put his hands on the inner sides of my knees, and pushed them apart as he struggled to enter me.

"No," I said, shoving him away, "I don't want to, not like this. Please stop, you're scaring me."

His laugh was harsh, "How could I scare you? You're the one who's not afraid of anything, remember? And if you're not afraid of dead men, why should you be frightened by me? I won't hurt you," his rough hands on my body belied his statement, "I just want to love you."

"No." I said it so softly that he couldn't have heard. But it echoed off the walls of the apartment, roaring in my head. Jonathan stopped groping and lifted his head, listening. A great blast of frigid air hit us, making me shiver uncontrollably. He stared at me in shock for a minute.

"No," I whispered to him in the darkness and the word roared back at us. The dishes in the cabinets began to clatter, the doors shook open, and glasses and plates began to fall and shatter.

Jonathan backed off, hastily pulling up his pants, not even stopping long enough to zip them up. "I'd better go now," he said, viewing the wreckage on the floor with terror, his hands grasping the waist of his pants, "I'll call…"

"No."

This time I did not need to say it; someone else said it for me. I heard the door slam as Jonathan left and looked around at the kitchen. The shaking subsided and I watched one final glass fall, as if in slow motion, and break apart on the floor.

My shoulders heaved and I slid off the counter. I couldn't tell at first whether I was crying or laughing. But when the deep, thrilling voice I'd heard before in my dreams began to laugh, I joined him, stunned and more than slightly hysterical, until tears streamed down my face.

"I guess that showed him, Owen," I whispered when my spasms had passed. "Thank you." I expected some sort of response from my ghostly defender, but there was nothing. The room felt empty and lonely. At that very moment the timer went off. I hit it with my hand, gave a half smile. "And, ladies and gentlemen, time's up."

Almost a week passed with no word from Jonathan and no sign of the presence that once occupied my apartment. I felt strangely deserted by both of them. I could easily understand Jonathan's attitude, why he didn't want to face me or the wrath waiting for him in my apartment. But where had Owen gone? He had been here; that evening with Jonathan had proved it. But just as certainly I knew that he was here no longer.

Maybe his work was done, I thought, maybe he redeemed his soul by saving me from Jonathan. "But that's probably a load of bull. And you'll never know, Mara," I said aloud, "so just forget about it."

But I found that I couldn't forget. The erotic dreams stopped as did the inspiration I'd received for my painting. I grew despondent and moody until it was all I could do to drag myself out of bed. One afternoon, after spending long, frustrating hours trying to finish the Apollo and Daphne canvas, I threw down my brushes in anger and flung myself onto the bed.

"You said you'd never leave me, that we'd be together forever," I cried to my invisible lover, "and then you left." I buried my head in the pillow. "Come back," I begged the emptiness, "come back to me. I want you. I love you."

Suddenly a warm spring breeze blew through the apartment; my breath caught in my throat and my tears subsided. The prisms on the chandelier sang their crystal songs again and the fragrance of flowers was intoxicating. Chandelier? I thought, and flowers? Ah, relief flooded my body, the dream again.

But when I rolled over, I knew that I was not asleep. The apartment wasn't filled with flowers, the furniture was mine, and the overhead light had no prisms to jingle in the air. But still I heard them and smelled the roses. My eyes went to the painting of Apollo and Daphne and once again the eyes of my canvas god met mine. I felt the thrill of his glance through my entire body, and when the figure moved and stepped off the canvas, I gasped. He laughed gently, and turned around to study the painting.

"A good likeness." His voice was deep, but slightly hollow at the same time, as if he was speaking to me from a long distance. "You have talent, my dear."

"Who are you?" My voice wavered slightly, this is not a dream, I reminded myself and my stomach tightened. I couldn't tell if it was fear or anticipation.

He turned back to me, and gave me a bow, graceful and courtly that did not seem incongruous even considering his lack of clothes. "You called and I came."

"Owen Culver?"

The movement of his head could have been a nod.

"But you're dead."

He didn't say anything, but crossed the room to me. His eyes burned on me and it became difficult for me to breath. It was as if he was draining the life from my body with his look. I knew he was and I didn't care. I reached up and unbuttoned my painting shirt, throwing it open and revealing my naked body to his stare. He smiled then, displaying teeth white and even. His cold hand reached down and delicately touched the skin of my stomach.

"Ah," I sighed and my body bucked slightly.

"You must ask me."

"Ask you?" I was confused at his hesitation. I wanted him so much. "Ask you what?"

"It is difficult for me to speak," the words fell slowly from his mouth, "I am sorry." He gave a small grimace then smiled again. "You must ask me to take you."

A flood of passion washed over my body, and a hot flush crept into my face. I hesitated for only a moment. "Yes," I whispered, shameless in my desire for him, "I want you. No one but you."

"Good." That one word from him was a vow, a promise and I knew deep in my soul that somehow my words had sealed a pact with him forever.

God help me, I thought as I studied the figure that hovered over me, *I love him. And I don't care who or what he is.*

Then he touched me again and my entire body seemed to explode into a blaze of desire. His mouth came down on mine, his lips were cold, but he kept them pressed to mine and I felt them grow warm. He was sucking the fire of my body into his. I wanted him to have it; there was nothing I would deny him.

I kept my eyes wide open, not wanting to miss the look of him. Everywhere his lips or his hands caressed, a small reddened patch would spring up, blossoming before my eyes like a delicate flower. There was no pain, only an excruciating ecstasy. I couldn't bear for it to continue and I couldn't bear for it to stop.

It might have been hours that I lay on the bed accepting his embraces and his icy kisses. Time, I knew, had no meaning for him and so it had no meaning for me. With mouth and tongue and hands, he explored every inch of my body. I grew so aroused that even the slightest touch anywhere would make me writhe and shudder. He didn't speak, he didn't need to. And I was long past speech.

I ached to touch him, to hold him tightly against me. Although with each passing minute, his limbs seemed to grow more substantial to my eyes and the weight of the body pressed to mine grew heavier, he was still out of reach, reminding me again and again that this was not a mortal man who held me in intimate embrace. Strangely, I was not frightened; this eeriness only intensified our lovemaking and his touch on me somehow became doubly precious because I could not return it.

And still his mouth and hands continued, coaxing me to the edge of despair, the brink of ecstasy. Finally, when I felt I could stand no more, he straddled me and gazed at me hungrily, his eyes blazing with the heat he had stolen from eager body.

"Yes," I breathed, reaching my arms up to him, feeling the contact of his body as no more than the delicate fingers of fog on naked skin.

He smiled, his fingers reached down and stoked my cheek gently. "Mara," he whispered and plunged into me, so desperately, so deeply. I screamed in excruciating pain. I never wanted it to end.

His penis was hard and unyielding like stone. Its invasion into the inferno of my vagina was an almost indescribable union of fire and ice, each element feeding the other endlessly. And it seemed endless. He withdrew and thrust repeatedly, and my body convulsed over and over, until my control broke down completely and I cried, writhing and shuddering, begging him to stop, begging him to never stop.

His thrusting grew more frenzied and as I watched, the outline of his ethereal body began to waver and dim. I could feel his moans start; a deep vibration that began in the very center of my being and echoed to my fingertips and my feet. My extremities hummed and buzzed with his pleasure and the hair on my head began to rise from the pillow and dance in the air.

Only when he exploded into me, did I finally close my eyes. As wild colors played behind my eyelids, I realized that I would die from his love. Not this time, perhaps, and not the next, but I would certainly die. And I realized too, regardless of this knowledge, that I would gladly give myself to him again.

His body collapsed on mine, crushing my bruised skin. I winced and smiled, feeling his breath touch my shoulder. When I opened my eyes he was not visible. But it no longer mattered; I was his forever. Even when I felt his presence depart, I knew he would return.

He did return, day after day, night after night, sometimes in dreams and sometimes during my waking hours. We did not make love again, and after several visits, I began to understand his limitations and the rules that governed his existence on this plane. He could speak, he could become visible, or he could exert his touch on living flesh. To manage all three at one time took tremendous effort and concentration.

I never knew how he would come to me, as a word breathed into my ear, a glimpse of his body out of the corner of my eye, or a gentle touch on my shoulder as I worked. Still, I knew he was with me and I was content.

"I would have you again."

I'd been putting the finishing touches on the Apollo canvas, when the words he breathed against my neck sent chills up my spine. My mouth twisted into a slow, sensual smile, I put my brush down and turned around only to be caught up in his invisible arms. "Hello, Owen," I said before his mouth covered mine.

He eased me down onto the floor of the studio and began to make love to me. His caresses were as intense and as unhurried as before, the only difference was that I could not see him. With my eyes closed, though, the remembered image of his face, his eyes, his magnificent body carried me deeper into frantic passion.

He entered me, I cried out in ecstasy. When my eyes flew open, they focused not on Owen, but on someone that should not have been there. I screamed again, this time in rage and fear. "Get out," I cried, still writhing under my lover. Owen's weight shifted on top of me, and I knew that he had turned his unseen eyes upon the face of the intruder.

"Get out," I screamed again, my voice hoarse, my throat aching.

Jonathan Weber stood over me, staring down unbelievingly at my shuddering body. I followed his gaze and saw my breasts flattened against an invisible chest, my pelvis rocked up and down violently on the tile floor by the thrusting of an invisible penis.

Jonathan's eyes opened wider, then he smiled, and began to unzip his pants, not understanding what he saw.

The blood in my veins turned to ice. *Oh, God,* I prayed, *let him understand. Let him leave.*

Owen continued his movements, more frantic and frenzied.

"Get out," I gasped between clenched teeth.

Jonathan laughed. "An interesting game, Mara," he said, slipping his pants off and idly stroking himself, "can two play?"

"Get out, you're not wanted here. Please, Jonathan, just leave now." Anything else I tried to say was lost in my final groans and the sounds of release that did not come from me. More than ever, I wanted to hold Owen to me, to prevent his anger. But as always he eluded my grasp and he pulled himself from me. I cried when I felt the pressure of his body lessen and disappear.

I met Jonathan's eyes, pleading with him. "Leave now, while you can. This isn't what you think, Jonathan, you don't understand."

"On the contrary, Mara," he said, lowering himself down on top of the body Owen had just left, "I understand quite well."

"No," I warned him. "Don't do this."

He laughed and shifted his weight so that he could enter me. I tried to scramble back away from him, but he grabbed my wrists and pinioned them to the floor. He smiled cruelly as he slammed into my already bruised body.

Suddenly the air in the apartment turned brutally cold and Jonathan began to choke.

I felt him wither inside me. His eyes were frantic with fear as his hands tried to loosen the invisible pressure on his neck. His body rose from mine. I quickly got up and ran to the corner of my bedroom, unable to believe what I saw.

Jonathan hung, suspended in mid-air, his legs kicking violently at something I knew he could not fight. His face paled and he coughed, bruises in the shape of long fingers appeared on his throat and his struggles grew less and less strenuous. Finally his limp body was flung across the room, where it hit the kitchen door frame. Over my frightened sobs, I could hear the sharp crack of bones breaking, and Jonathan collapsed into an almost unrecognizable bundle of skin and bones. His staring eyes glazed over and blood gushed briefly from his nose and his mouth, his last breath visible in the frigid air. When it stopped, I was alone again, naked, bruised and screaming uncontrollably in the night.

So they put me here, where all I do is tell my story over and over again to doctors who merely nod, jotting endless notes on endless pages. They think I'm crazy; they think I'm a freak. It doesn't matter, nothing matters except for the fact that he's with me here, where no living man could ever enter. His promise to me, unlike all the others of my life, turned out to be true. He will never leave this plane of existence until I'm ready to leave with him.

I stroke my expanding stomach, softly, gently, knowing that it's the only touch I'll ever give to his child. That saddens me, I'd always wanted a baby. But Owen is beckoning to me, and when Owen calls for the last time, I'll go to him.

"Soon," I whisper to him across the room where he stands, watching and waiting. The doctors shake their heads and smirk at my supposed insanity. I merely smile, rocking back and forth on my chair. "I'll come soon, my love."